ANDREW LOST

BY J. C. GREENBURG

ILLUSTRATED
BY DEBBIE PALEN

1 ON THE DOG

A STEPPING STONE BOOK™

Random House New York

Text copyright © 2002 by J. C. Greenburg. Illustrations copyright © 2002 by Debbie Palen. All rights reserved under International and Pan-American Copyright Conventions. Published in the United States by Random House Children's Books, a division of Random House, Inc., New York, and simultaneously in Canada by Random House of Canada Limited, Toronto.

www.randomhouse.com/kids
www.AndrewLost.com

Library of Congress Cataloging-in-Publication Data
Greenburg, J. C. (Judith C.)
Andrew lost. On the dog / by J. C. Greenburg ;
illustrated by Debbie Palen.   p.   cm. — (A Stepping stone book)
SUMMARY: When ten-year-old Andrew invents a shrinking machine, he does not expect to be sucked into the machine along with his cousin Judy, only to end up in a dog's nose.
ISBN 0-375-81277-6 (trade) — ISBN 0-375-91277-0 (lib. bdg.)
[1. Inventions—Fiction.   2. Size—Fiction.   3. Dogs—Fiction.
4. Cousins—Fiction.]   I. Title: Andrew lost.   II. Title: On the dog.
III. Palen, Debbie, ill.   IV. Title.   V. Series.
PZ7.G82785 An 2002   [Fic]—dc21   2001048713

Printed in the United States of America
First Edition May 2002   10 9 8 7 6

RANDOM HOUSE and colophon are registered trademarks and A STEPPING STONE BOOK and colophon are trademarks of Random House, Inc. ANDREW LOST is a trademark of J. C. Greenburg.

*To Dan and Zack and Dad
and the real Andrew, with love.
—J.C.G.*

*For Sid, the cat who acted like a dog.
—D.P.*

CONTENTS

ANDREW LOST

ON THE DOG

ANDREW'S WORLD

Andrew Dubble

Andrew has been inventing things since he was four. His first invention was the Whoops Eraser. It was supposed to get rid of stains. But it also got rid of the things that *had* the stains. The Picker Upper picked up spills. But then it leaked them out again.

Andrew is ten now. Today he's trying out his newest invention, the Atom Sucker.

Judy Dubble

Judy is Andrew's thirteen-year-old cousin. Judy has been on four safaris to Africa. She's got a helicopter in her backyard. She even knows how to fly it!

The Atom Sucker

Is it possible to shrink something by sucking the space out of its atoms? Andrew thinks the answer is yes and his Atom Sucker can do it. But he's been wrong before.

Uncle Al

Uncle Al works at a top-secret laboratory. No one knows what he really does there. But Andrew and Judy know he's very smart and gives good presents!

Thudd

The Handy Ultra-Digital Detective. On

Andrew's seventh birthday, Thudd turned up in Andrew's mailbox. A card was hanging from one of Thudd's antennas. It said: HAPPY BIRTHDAY, ANDREW! TAKE GOOD CARE OF THUDD. HE CAN TELL YOU EVERY-THING. LOVE, UNCLE AL. P.S. *NEVER* WASH THUDD AND DON'T KEEP HIM IN THE DARK!

Mrs. Scuttle

Mrs. Scuttle is Judy's next-door neigh-bor. There aren't many things Mrs. Scuttle likes. She doesn't even like her dog, Harley, very much.

Harley

Mrs. Scuttle may own this basset hound, but Judy throws him Frisbees and buys him chew toys. Judy and Harley are close friends. They are about to get *much* closer!

THE
ATOM
SUCKER
THE MOST
POWERFUL
SHRINKER
IN THE
UNIVERSE

THE ATOM SUCKER

"Wowzers!" Andrew shouted. "This is the best thing I've ever invented!"

Ten-year-old Andrew Dubble parked his new machine under a tree. The machine was as big as a doghouse. It looked like a porcupine. Skinny copper tubes poked out all over it. A fat iron pipe stuck out from the front.

The machine squatted on four big springs. A thick electrical cord hung from the back like a tail.

On the fat iron pipe, Andrew had painted the words THE ATOM SUCKER. In smaller letters he had written THE MOST POWERFUL SHRINKER IN THE UNIVERSE!

Andrew dragged the plug to the back porch of an old white house. Andrew's thirteen-year-old cousin Judy Dubble lived here with her parents. But nobody was home on this sunny summer day. Andrew had the field behind the house all to himself.

Andrew plugged in the Atom Sucker. Then he walked back to the machine to set the controls.

On the back of the Atom Sucker were a black power dial and a big red switch. The dial set the shrinking power from 0 to 100. Moving the dial past 0 turned the Atom Sucker on. The red switch could be pushed up or down. Up was marked SHRINK. Down was marked UN-SHRINK.

Andrew pushed the big red switch up to SHRINK. Then he turned the power dial up to 5—low shrinking power.

The Atom Sucker began to wobble. The skinny tubes began to twirl. Soon they were whistling like a hundred teakettles.

"Super-duper pooper-scooper!" Andrew shouted. "What should I shrink first?"

He looked around the fenced-in field. Judy's parents kept equipment for their adventure-travel business here.

At the far end of the field was an airplane with just four seats. A silver speedboat leaned against the fence. A helicopter was parked in front of the tree where the Atom Sucker sat.

"The helicopter!" Andrew smiled. *"Yes!"*

meep . . . "Drewd! Noop!" came a squeaky little voice from Andrew's pants pocket.

Andrew looked down. "What's the matter, Thudd?" he asked.

Sticking out of Andrew's front pocket was a little silver robot. Andrew's Uncle Al, a top-secret scientist, had invented him. The robot's official name was The Handy Ultra-Digital

Detective. But Andrew called him Thudd for
short.

Thudd's face was a video screen. His ears
were two antennas. On Thudd's chest were
three rows of buttons. All the buttons glowed
green except for one. The big button in the
center glowed purple.

Thudd had three fingers on each hand. Thudd was using all his fingers to hang on to the top of Andrew's pocket. Thudd's rubbery little feet were like jelly beans with flat bottoms. They were kicking the keys in Andrew's pocket.

meep . . . "Copter too big!" said Thudd. "Atom Sucker choke maybe! Explode maybe! Small thing first, please!"

Thudd made the keys jangle in Andrew's pocket.

"Okay, okay," Andrew said. "Calm down. Let's go see if there's something good in the garbage."

Leaning against the porch were a garbage can and a lumpy black bag. It smelled stinky. Andrew lifted the lid of the garbage can. Inside were empty paint cans, sticky brushes, and an old radio. Andrew pulled the radio out.

"How about this?" Andrew asked.

meep . . . "Good! Good! Good!" said Thudd.

Andrew fiddled with the radio as he walked back to the Atom Sucker.

meep . . . "Drewd! Stay way from big pipe!" said Thudd.

"Whoops!" said Andrew. "Thanks, Thudd."

The fat iron pipe at the front of the Atom Sucker was where the shrinking was supposed to happen. The pipe was snorting and wagging from side to side. It was looking for something to shrink!

meep . . . "No shrink us, please!" Thudd squeaked.

"Don't worry," said Andrew. "*I'm* not worried."

meep . . . "Worried!" said Thudd.

Andrew crouched behind the Atom Sucker. He double-checked the controls.

"Ready."

He raised the radio over his head.

"Set."

He tossed it toward the front of the machine.

"Go!"

A cloud of orange smoke whooshed out of the twirling copper tubes.

SHNOOOOORP! snorted the Atom Sucker.

Andrew couldn't see the radio through the orange smoke. He couldn't see anything at all. But he could hear a scream.

A LITTLE MISTAKE

"Cheese Louise!" It was Andrew's cousin Judy.

meep . . . "Oody here!" Thudd squeaked. "Hiya, Oody!"

"Ah . . . *choof!*" Judy sneezed. "What *is* all this stinky smoke?"

"It's just my science project," Andrew said. He turned the Atom Sucker's power dial down to 0. "You said I could come over and work on it."

"I said you could come over and use my *printer!*" Judy said. She stomped toward Andrew. Her long, frizzy hair bounced with every step. "I *didn't* say you could explode stuff in my backyard!"

Woof!

Harley the basset hound trotted over to them. Harley belonged to Judy's neighbor Mrs. Scuttle. But Harley followed Judy everywhere.

"Nothing exploded . . . probably," Andrew said.

Judy bent down to scratch Harley behind one of his long brown ears.

"Ah . . . ah . . . ah . . . *choof!*" Judy sneezed again. "This smoke is awful for my allergies, and so is Harley."

Harley snuffled in the grass, then trotted away.

"Listen, Andrew," said Judy. "Mom and Dad are teaching a skydiving class today. If I let you wreck things while they're gone, they'll never let me help with the tour to Hawaii. I'm supposed to teach people how to swim with dolphins!"

"All I did was shrink a broken radio," Andrew said. "At least I *think* I shrunk it."

Judy folded her arms across her chest. Judy was only an inch taller than Andrew. But sometimes she seemed a lot taller.

"Mrs. Carmody assigned us a science

report on ants," Andrew explained. "I figured if I could get *inside* an anthill, I could *really* understand them. So Thudd helped me build the Atom Sucker. It can shrink us down to any size."

"Oh, *please,* Andrew!" said Judy. "Not another crazy invention!"

"But this one is *amazing*!" said Andrew.

"Yeah, right," said Judy. "That's what you said about the Aroma-Rama. Our house smelled like stinky feet for weeks!"

Judy walked over to the Atom Sucker. The smoke was clearing away.

"So how does this stupid thing work?" she asked.

"Well," said Andrew, "atoms are almost all empty space. The Atom Sucker sucks the empty space out of atoms. When your *atoms* shrink, *you* shrink!"

Woof!

Harley ran over to Judy. He had a Frisbee

in his mouth. Judy patted Harley and tossed the Frisbee toward the far end of the field. Harley bounded after it.

"Help me find the radio," said Andrew. "It should be somewhere in front of the big pipe."

meep . . . "Stay way from big pipe!" warned Thudd.

"It's okay, Thudd," Andrew said. "I turned the power off."

Andrew got down on his hands and knees and started looking around in the grass. Judy did, too.

meep . . . "There, Drewd!" Thudd said. He pointed toward a tree root.

Andrew picked up the radio. It was the size of a matchbook.

"Yes!" he shouted.

"Let me see that," said Judy. She took the little radio from Andrew's hand.

"Wow! It's perfect!" she said. "But how

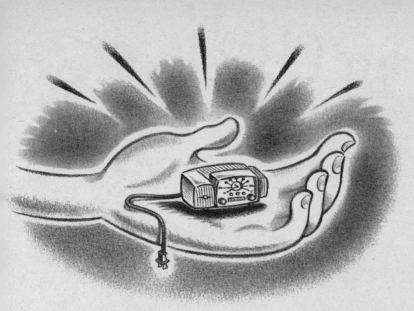

are you going to get it *un*-shrunk?"

"I'll just set the Atom Sucker to UN-SHRINK," said Andrew. "It'll blow the radio right back up again."

Judy frowned. "I'm allergic to sentences with the words 'blow up' in them."

"Just watch this," said Andrew.

He hurried to the Atom Sucker's controls and turned the power dial up to 5.

The skinny copper tubes twirled and whistled. The fat iron pipe started wagging.

Andrew was about to push the red switch to UN-SHRINK when Thudd screamed.

"Oody!"

Andrew looked up. Judy was near the front of the Atom Sucker. She was in the middle of a sneeze.

"Ah . . . ah . . . *choof!*"

Andrew jumped. His hand hit the power dial. It spun all the way up to 100!

The Atom Sucker started hopping like a crazed kangaroo.

Judy looked up. Her eyes were as round as golf balls.

SHLOOOOORP! the Atom Sucker bellowed.

There was a cloud of orange smoke where Judy used to be.

"Noop! Noop! Noop!" squeaked Thudd.

The Atom Sucker hopped toward the helicopter.

SKLUUUUURP!

The helicopter was gone!

"Oh, no!" Andrew cried.

He tried to pull the plug. He jerked on the cord. The Atom Sucker spun toward *him*!

Out of the corner of his eye, Andrew saw Harley running across the yard.

"Go back, Harley!" Andrew yelled.

Suddenly Andrew felt as if he were being tickled by monkeys and squashed into a suitcase.

The last thing he heard was a booming *SHLOOOOORP!*

3 NOSING AROUND

"Yowzers!" Andrew yelled.

It was dark. A cool wind was blowing. In the wind were little chunks of stuff. They smacked into Andrew as they flew by.

Where am I? Andrew thought.

Ahead of him Andrew could see a faraway dot of light. Behind him was an even darker darkness.

Andrew's head felt weird and heavy. *I know what this feeling is!* Andrew thought. *I'm hanging upside down, like a bat in a cave!*

Andrew tried to move his feet, but they

were stuck in goo. The wind was so strong it was sucking him through the goo, back into the darker darkness!

Andrew reached out for something to hold on to. Strange sticky ropes were hanging down all around him. He grabbed one.

"Judy!" Andrew yelled.

meep . . . "Dark, dark, dark, Drewd!" said Thudd. "Fraid of dark!"

Andrew pulled Thudd out of his pocket. It was good to see Thudd's bright screen, even though there was a frown on it.

The wind slowed down. A moment later, it whipped up again. But this time the wind was hot and damp, and going the other way. It pushed Andrew toward the dot of light.

"Can you tell where we are, Thudd?" asked Andrew, holding on tight to a rope.

Thudd's buttons were blinking yellow. Thudd was upset!

meep . . . "Harley!" Thudd announced.

"You mean we're on the *dog*?" asked Andrew.

meep . . . "*In* Harley," said Thudd. "In Harley's nose!"

"Holy moly!" said Andrew. "We must be *really* small!"

meep . . . "I show you," said Thudd.

Thudd's face disappeared from his screen. In its place appeared a picture of Andrew. The picture began to shrink. First it shrank to the size of a pencil eraser, then to a dot, then to nothing.

Andrew felt a little dizzy. Partly it was from being upside down. But mostly it was from thinking about how small he was.

Andrew slipped Thudd back into his front pants pocket.

"Grab the cord that holds my keys, Thudd," said Andrew. "Wrap it around yourself so you won't fall out."

meep . . . "Okey-dokey," said Thudd.

Then Andrew reached for his mini-flashlight. He always attached it to his belt loop. Andrew unhooked the flashlight and turned it on.

The flashlight's bright yellow beam sliced through the darkness of the nose cave. It was a huge place!

The roof of the nose was as wrinkled as a messy bedsheet. Zillions of gooey ropes hung down from the folds.

The bottom of the nose was far below. It looked gooey down there, too.

Suddenly the sides of the nose cave started moving in and out quickly. The

dog-breath wind came in short little gusts.

meep . . . "Harley smell something," said Thudd. "Dog nose smell things million times better than human nose. Harley can find place where Drewd walked four days ago. Can find Drewd buried under snow. Can tell if Drewd happy or sad by how Drewd smell."

"I know Uncle Al programmed you to tell me everything you know about everything," said Andrew. "But right now we've got to concentrate on finding Judy."

Just then, Harley gave a big, gusty sniff.

4 A STICKY SITUATION

"Ick!" came a voice in the darkness.

"Judy!" Andrew shouted.

"Andrew!" Judy shouted back.

Andrew turned off his flashlight and snapped it back on to his belt loop. He grabbed the sticky ropes with both hands and started pulling himself through the goo toward Judy's voice.

"Ouch!" Judy yelled.

"Oof!" Andrew hollered.

Judy and Andrew had clunked heads.

"Andrew!" Judy gasped. "First I land on a

gigantic blade of grass. Then Harley's nose hovers over me like a humongous spaceship! Next he's sniffing me up! Now because of you and your stupid Atom Sucker, I'm soaked in nose goo!"

meep . . . "Nose goo called mucus," said Thudd. "Gooey mucus *good*! If nose not gooey, nose not smell. Tiny pieces come off everything that have smell."

Thudd pointed to a picture on his face screen.

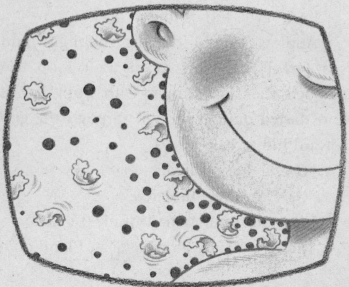

"Tiny pieces stick to gooey nose cells," Thudd said. "Look!"

Thudd pointed to a new picture on his face screen.

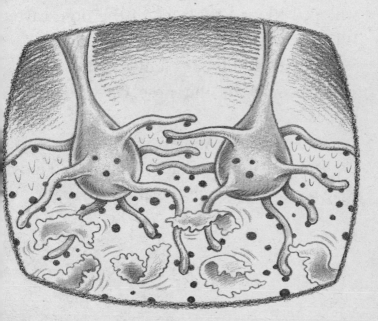

"Nose cells send message to dog brain. 'Dead squirrel. Yummy! New dog. Nasty! Oody. Friend!' Harley find Oody cuz he got lotsa gooey nose cells!"

Judy frowned. "If I hear one more word about nose goo, I'll take out your batteries, Thudd!"

Just then, a huge gust of dog-breath wind whipped toward the back of the nose cave. When it stopped, everything got quiet.

"What's going on?" Judy asked.

The walls of the nose cave began to quiver.

"Uh-oh," said Andrew.

There was an explosion. Andrew and Judy were blasting through the air!

UPS AND DOWNS

"Yeow!" Andrew screamed.

He crashed into something rubbery.

"Yoof!"

Andrew squinted. It was very bright. The light hurt his eyes after the darkness of the nose.

"Thudd, what happened?" he asked.

meep . . . "Harley sneeze!" said Thudd. "Sneeze can go one hundred miles an hour— fast as tornado!"

Andrew's eyes started to get used to the light. It looked as if they were at the mouth of an enormous cave. They were stuck to the very top of it.

Suddenly Andrew knew where they were.

"We're at the end of Harley's nose," said Andrew, "at the top of Harley's nostril!"

meep . . . "Drewd! Look!" Thudd said. "Oody's fingers!"

"Where?" asked Andrew.

meep . . . "Down!" said Thudd.

Way below, Judy was dangling by her fingertips from the bottom edge of Harley's nostril.

"Help!" she screamed. "I can't hold on much longer!"

Suddenly a pink tidal wave curled up toward Judy. It was Harley's tongue! It was covered with gigantic bristles, like a monster hairbrush.

"Look out!" Andrew shouted.

Judy screamed. The tongue picked her up and swooped her toward Andrew.

Andrew reached out to grab Judy as the tongue went by. But all Andrew got were wet tongue bristles. Then the tongue swooped back into Harley's mouth.

meep . . . "Oody gone!" cried Thudd.

"*Almost* gone!" a voice gasped from above. "I'm on top of Harley's nose. Andrew, get out of that nostril and get up here!"

Andrew leaned out of the nostril and

looked up. Getting to the top of Harley's nose would be like climbing a craggy black cliff.

Andrew tucked Thudd into his back pocket and started to climb. The front of Harley's nose was covered with pits and cracks. Andrew used them to grab on to.

Being sticky with nose goo helped.

I feel like a fly walking up a wall, Andrew thought. *Maybe I can use this nose goo stuff in one of my inventions!*

Finally, Andrew scrambled over the edge of the nose. It felt good to be somewhere flat, even if it was the top of a dog's nose.

meep . . . "Want to see, please," said Thudd.

Andrew put Thudd into his shirt pocket.

Ahead was a strange sight. It looked like a blown-down forest of scaly tree trunks. But it was really thousands of dog hairs all leaning in one direction.

Judy was leaning against one of the hairs.

On her face was a "wait till I get my hands on you" look.

Andrew looked over the edge of the nose cliff.

"This nose could *really* use a safety railing," he said.

"This is *not* funny," Judy said.

Suddenly everything spun to the right. Andrew was glad he was still sticky. He was too sticky to fall off the nose!

"Harley must be getting ready to take a nap!" Judy said. She was clinging to one of the dog hairs. "He always turns around and around first."

Finally, Harley curled up in the shade. Harley's sigh rumbled below them like an underground train.

Judy and Andrew sat down at the edge of the dog-hair forest.

"So how do we get un-shrunk?" Judy asked.

"We set the Atom Sucker to UN-SHRINK," said Andrew. "We have eight hours from when I turned it on."

"What happens if we don't get back in eight hours?" asked Judy.

Andrew looked away. "Um . . . the Atom Sucker might kind of . . . explode."

A PLAN?

"*What?*" Judy yelled.

"Don't worry," said Andrew. "Thudd, what time did I turn on the Atom Sucker?"

meep . . . "12:01," said Thudd.

"So all we have to do is set it to UN-SHRINK before 8:01," Andrew said.

meep . . . "Now 12:31," said Thudd. "Only 7 hours, 30 minutes left."

"Cheese Louise!" said Judy. "We'd better come up with a plan!"

meep . . . "Purple button!" said Thudd, pointing to the middle of his chest.

"A purple button is *not* a plan," said Judy.

meep . . . "Purple button send signal to Uncle Al," said Thudd.

"I think Uncle Al is setting up a telescope to look into space," said Andrew. "I sure hope he can get our signal."

Thudd pressed his purple button. It blinked three times.

"How will we know if the signal reaches Uncle Al?" asked Judy.

meep . . . "Not know," said Thudd. "Purple button never pressed before."

"Well, we'd better not sit around waiting for Uncle Al to come get us," said Judy. "We need to get off the dog, across the field, and onto the Atom Sucker."

Judy got up and looked around. "I don't see the helicopter," she said.

"It got shrunk right after you did," said Andrew.

Judy snapped her fingers. "That's it! If

we can find the helicopter, I can fly it!"

"We all ended up on Harley," said Andrew. "Maybe the helicopter is on Harley, too!"

"Let's hike to the top of Harley's head," said Judy. "Maybe we can spot the helicopter from up there."

Andrew looked up. A long, furry slope led from the tip of Harley's nose to the brown mountain of Harley's head.

"Okay," said Andrew. "It's time to climb!"

Andrew took a step into the dog-hair forest.

"Oops!" Andrew yelped. His feet slid out from under him. "It's slippery!"

Judy crouched down to look at the bottom of a dog hair.

"All the hairs are growing out of these big round pits in Harley's skin," said Judy. "They're like trees growing in pots. And the pits are full of oil. Eew! I can really smell that doggie smell!"

meep . . . "Hair pit called follicle," said Thudd. "Follicle make oil. Oil protect skin and hair. No oil, skin crack. Hair break. But when oil get old, oil get stinky. Like bad milk. That why dog smell good after bath. Stinky oil get washed away."

Oil gland

Hair follicle

Judy pulled Andrew back to his feet. They started hiking up Harley's nose. The dog hairs curved over them like the trunks of giant palm trees. Sunlight flickered down through the hairs to Harley's skin.

Harley's skin was covered with stuff that looked like torn-up tissue paper. Pieces floated into the air as Andrew and Judy shuffled along.

"What *is* this stuff?" Andrew asked.

meep . . . "Skin flakes," Thudd said. "Old skin peel off animals. Millions and millions of flakes every day. Drewd and Oody make skin flakes, too!"

"Maybe Andrew does," said Judy. "But *I* don't."

meep . . . "Dust mostly skin flakes," said Thudd.

Judy laughed. "So those piles of dust in Andrew's room are really piles of Andrew?"

"Yoop!" said Thudd. "Know what eat skin flakes?"

"A vacuum cleaner!" said Andrew.

meep . . . "Dust mites!" said Thudd, pointing to a picture on his face screen. "Tiny bugs. Live in rugs. On sheets. On clothes. Dust mites love skin flakes like Drewd love pizza!"

Up ahead, Andrew saw a huge brown dome.

"It's Harley's eyelid!" said Andrew. "We're halfway there."

Harley's skin was warm, and the hike past Harley's eye was steep and slippery. When they got above the eye, Judy and Andrew stopped for a rest.

"It's not far now," said Andrew.

He leaned out to get another look at Harley's eye.

"Wowzers!" said Andrew. "Harley's eyeball is moving under his eyelid."

Andrew wanted to get a better look, so he leaned out a little bit farther. But that was a little bit *too* far.

MITE-Y BIG PROBLEMS

"Nooooo!" Andrew screamed. He tumbled down Harley's eyelid and crashed into one of his eyelashes.

"Are you okay?" Judy shouted down.

"I think so," said Andrew. He tried to get to his feet. But he started sinking!

"Help!" Andrew hollered.

meep . . . "Deep eyelash follicle!" said Thudd.

Before Andrew could do anything, he was up to his waist in an oil pit!

"I'm coming!" Judy yelled.

Andrew pulled Thudd out of his pocket to keep him out of the oil. With his other hand, Andrew grabbed the edge of the follicle. But it was too slippery to get a grip.

Judy climbed down Harley's eyelid and crawled to the edge of the follicle.

Andrew's head was bobbing just above the oil!

"Yikes!" Andrew cried. "There's something slithering around in here! It feels like this pit is full of snakes!"

meep . . . "Eyelash mites," Thudd said. "Eyelash mites live upside down in follicle. Eat oil and skin flakes. Humans got eyelash mites, too. See!"

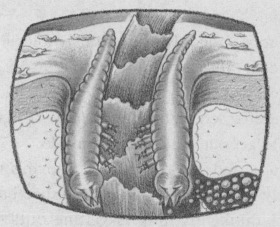

"I've got to get out of here before these mites think I'm a skin flake!" said Andrew.

Judy grabbed Andrew's hand and tried to yank him out.

She groaned. "You sure are heavy," she

said. "I can pull better if I stand up. Whoops!"

Judy slipped and tumbled into the follicle.

"Yikes!" she yelped. "I got pinched!"

meep . . . "Eyelash mites got claws," said Thudd. "Cousins of lobsters!"

"Do these stupid mites ever leave a follicle?" asked Judy.

"Yoop," said Thudd. "When follicle too crowded, mites leave."

"So let's make this follicle feel like an overstuffed school bus!" said Judy. "If a mite tries to get out, we can hitch a ride."

Judy and Andrew started shoving their prickly neighbors. The mites thrashed back.

"I think this mite is getting out!" said Andrew.

Andrew wrapped his arms around the slippery tail of the mite next to him. It squirmed tail-first toward the top of the follicle.

"Grab on to me, Judy!" said Andrew.
Judy caught hold of Andrew's belt.

The eyelash mite gave another squirm and slithered out onto Harley's eyelid. Judy and Andrew flopped off the mite. It wriggled over to another follicle.

"Woofers!" said Andrew. "That was awful!"

"That's the first time you've been right today," said Judy.

Judy and Andrew picked up some soft skin flakes and started wiping the oil off themselves.

Thudd grabbed on to Andrew's shirt and pinched his way back into Andrew's shirt pocket.

"Ah . . . ah . . . ah-*choof!*" Judy sneezed. "It's my dog allergy."

meep . . . "Bless oo!" said Thudd. "Oody not lergic to whole dog. Oody lergic to skin flakes and these."

Thudd pointed to the scales on the hairs. Some of them had cracked off. Hair scales were floating into the air with the skin flakes.

Judy looked up at Harley's head.

"I've got an idea," she said. "This time, let's do what mountain climbers do."

Judy took off her belt and threaded it through one of the loops on her jeans. Andrew looped his belt the same way. Then Judy buckled the ends of the two belts together.

"Now if one of us starts to fall, the other one can help," said Judy.

It was a hard climb from Harley's eye to the top of his head. Andrew and Judy had to pull themselves up hair by hair.

They were almost there when something crashed nearby.

Wham!

The forest of dog hairs rustled. Something big was coming!

TIME TO FLEA

An instant later, it was above them. Its claws gripped the tops of the dog hairs. Above the claws, six long legs bristled with sharp hairs.

One by one, the legs slipped down to Harley's skin. Andrew and Judy ran. But one of the legs caught the belts that held them together. They were trapped!

Andrew looked up. A huge armored creature towered over them. Pointy hairs stuck out all over its body. A snout hung down in front. It was a sharp, prickly snout!

Above the snout were two black cannonball eyes.

meep . . . "Flea!" Thudd said. "Flea not see Drewd and Judy. Flea not see much. But flea feel living thing move. Flea jump on! Flea need blood to live."

The flea lowered its needle-sharp snout-mouth to Harley's skin. Andrew and Judy yanked at their belts, trying to get free.

Maybe the flea felt something. Instead of biting Harley, it jumped! Up and up they went! Andrew had the feeling in his stomach that he got when an airplane took off.

The wind whooshed by their faces. It was scary to see how high they were!

meep . . . "If human jump like flea, human jump six hundred feet high!" Thudd squeaked.

Then they were zooming down, down, down! They could see the top of Harley's head and the furry brown hilltops of his ears.

"Hold on, Andrew!" screamed Judy. "We're going to crash!"

The flea landed on top of Harley's head. Andrew and Judy were jolted loose from the flea's leg. They tumbled down through the hairs to Harley's skin.

A dark shadow passed over them as the flea crept along the hairs above.

"Let's head for Harley's ear," said Judy. "It's high, so we can look around. And if anything nasty comes along, we can hide inside. I'll bet it's like a big cave in there."

Judy and Andrew trudged through the dog hair. Suddenly Andrew felt like he was on an elevator going up! Harley wasn't sleeping anymore. He was on the move. And so were his ears!

A HAIRY SITUATION

Harley's ears were going up like enormous furry tents!

"What's going on?" asked Andrew, looking up through the dog hairs.

meep . . . "Harley move ears to find where sound come from," said Thudd. "Dog ears like antennas."

Andrew listened. The only sound he heard was the Atom Sucker. It was whistling softly.

meep . . . "Harley hear something coming," said Thudd. "Dog ears hear better than Drewd ears. Human use mostly eyes to find out things. Dog use mostly nose and ears. Dog eyes see things blurry. See just yellow, blue, gray."

"*Grrrrr!*" Harley growled.

"I wonder what he's growling about," said Andrew. "If I climb to the tip of a hair, maybe I can see what's going on."

Andrew unbuckled the belts that held them together.

The scales on the hair made it easy to climb.

From the top of Harley's head, Andrew saw a strange sight. The forest of hair on the back of Harley's neck was standing straight up!

meep . . . "Harley scared!" Thudd said. "Muscles in skin make hair stick out. Happen to humans, too. Called goose bumps! Lotsa hair make animal look big, look scary! But humans not got enough hair to look scary."

"I think I see what Harley's growling at!" Andrew shouted down to Judy. "A very long puppy just came up to the fence."

"That must be Hot Dog!" Judy shouted up. "He just moved in with the Greenes across the street from us. They're *so* nice, especially Josh. His birthday is two days before mine."

A dreamy smile stretched across Judy's face.

"Now Hot Dog is sniffing the fence!"

yelled Andrew. "You know, where Harley always pees."

meep . . . "Harley smell on fence tell all about Harley to other dogs," said Thudd. "Smell tell if Harley male or female. Tell if Harley boss dog or shy dog."

Harley kept growling. He hunched down low to the ground and crept toward the puppy.

"Harley is right in front of Hot Dog now," said Andrew. "He's putting one of his front paws on Hot Dog's shoulder."

meep . . . "Harley say he boss dog," said Thudd.

"Now Hot Dog is rolling over on his back," Andrew reported.

meep . . . "Hot Dog agree. Harley boss dog," said Thudd.

Harley started wagging his tail. Hot Dog got up and wagged his tail, too.

meep . . . "Dogs need to know who boss,"

said Thudd. "Hot Dog and Harley friends now."

The hairs on Harley's neck leaned back down again.

As Andrew climbed down the hair to Harley's skin, a shadow fluttered overhead.

It was an orange-and-black butterfly. Harley and Hot Dog trotted after it.

"Yuck!" said Judy. "Something smells gross."

"It's probably the garbage bag by the porch," said Andrew. "I saw Harley sniffing it."

"Oh, no!" cried Judy. "We've got to get into Harley's ear right away!"

They ran. Andrew slipped on an oily patch. He almost fell into a hair follicle. They were still far away from the huge flaps of Harley's ears when it happened.

BATHTUB OF DOOM

"Holy moly!" said Andrew. Harley was diving like a roller coaster. Andrew and Judy grabbed a dog hair and hung on.

Then the roller coaster turned into the worst kind of water ride. Blobs of slimy eggs rained down on them. Boulders of stinky cheese flew through the air. Andrew and Judy nearly drowned in a glob of sour milk.

"I *knew* this was going to happen!" said Judy. "Harley loves to get into garbage bags. He rolls around in all the yucky stuff!"

"Why would Harley do a dumb thing like that?" asked Andrew.

meep . . . "Not dumb," said Thudd. "Long ago, dogs live wild. Dog need to hunt other animals. But other animals smell dog and run away. Dog roll in stinky stuff. Stinky stuff hide doggie smell. Now dog get food from food bowl, but dog still roll in stinky stuff."

"What on earth is going on?" boomed a woman's voice. "Harley! Get over here!"

"It's Mrs. Scuttle!" Judy gasped.

HARLEY!

"You bad dog!" yelled Mrs. Scuttle. "You're filthy! And what a stink!"

Mrs. Scuttle got quiet for a moment. "Where's that whistling coming from?" she said. "And what is *that* thing?"

"Oh my gosh!" said Judy. "She must have seen the Atom Sucker!"

"I hope she doesn't turn it off!" said Andrew.

"Another noisy gadget," snorted Mrs. Scuttle. "We've got to get those Dubbles out of the neighborhood."

Andrew chuckled. "If Mrs. Scuttle gets close to the Atom Sucker, she could end up in *our* neighborhood."

Judy laughed. "I'd rather have an eyelash mite for a neighbor."

Mrs. Scuttle's hand zoomed down and grabbed Harley's collar.

"Ooooow!" Harley whined.

"We have to get inside Harley's ear!" said

Judy. "Before we drown in Mrs. Scuttle's bath-tub."

Dog hair by dog hair, they pulled them-selves onto Harley's ear. But the ear was flapping like a giant rubbery flag. They couldn't get inside.

Mrs. Scuttle dragged Harley to her house. She battled him up the stairs and into the bathroom. The bathroom was as white as an igloo, except for the shower curtain. It was blue and had mermaids and pirate ships all over it.

"What time is it, Thudd?" Andrew asked.

meep . . . "1:57," said Thudd.

Judy and Andrew watched Mrs. Scuttle slide the shower curtain open and turn on the faucet.

"Thudd, did you hear anything from Uncle Al yet?" Andrew asked.

meep . . . "Noop," said Thudd.

Water roared into the tub.

"Sounds like Niagara Falls," said Andrew.

Mrs. Scuttle poured something into the water. Hot steam curled up into the room.

"Get in there, Harley!" Mrs. Scuttle thundered. Judy and Andrew hung on as Mrs. Scuttle pushed Harley over the edge of the tub.

meep . . . "Drewd!" called Thudd from Andrew's shirt pocket. "If Thudd get washed down drain, Thudd want to say Drewd been good friend. Thunkoo."

Sploosh!

Harley tumbled into the tub. An ocean of sudsy water rushed toward them.

I can't believe we're going to get washed down a drain like an old scab, thought Andrew. *Wait a minute. . . .*

Andrew reached into his front pocket. What he was looking for wasn't there.

I was pretty sure I had some, he thought. *Could it be in my back pocket? Yes!*

Andrew felt a small cube wrapped in paper.

Now we've got a chance!

TO BE CONTINUED IN

Andrew Lost in the Bathroom!